去られるために
去るために

Okutsu Sachiyo
奥津さちよ詩集

土曜美術社出版販売

詩集 去られるために 去るために ＊ 目次

I

ロンド 8

途上 12

ピーナッツ 15

息 18

雨あがり 21

ハクモクレン 24

松ぼっくり 26

ダンゴムシ 28

波乗り 30

II

いわし雲 34

今なら　もっと 37

黒い魚 40

麦 42

赤い時間 45

チェリーの頃 48

ヴィヴィール（生きよう） 50

インディアン村のごみ缶 53

テキーラ・ツアー 56

Ⅲ

ペダルを踏む 62

ひらひらと 65

スプリング 68

高い空 71

五月十七日 74

光る甲虫　77

鋭い冬が　79

冬のあいだに　82

「去られるために　そこにいる」　85

ふきのとう　88

＊

To Be Left and to Leave（英訳詩二十三篇）　146

あとがき　148

詩集

去られるために　去るために

I

ロンド

痛みで
ソファーに寝ころんでいる
すると　午後
淡いひかりがやってくる
かげろうのような
さざめいて
濃くなって　のびたりちぢんだり
だんだら模様の　ひかりのこども
壁は　あかるくなって

棚の古いラジオや
掛け時計の
それぞれの
顔の輪郭がくっきりと生きかえる

この冬に
南側の土地のさかいめに
かまぼこ型のビニールハウスが建てられ
視界はさえぎられ
公園の小さな木は見えなくなってしまったが
そのビニールハウスの
屋根から
フレームの出っ張りから
ひょいと　一直線にやってきてくれた

ひかりのこども
窓をあけている
かぐわしいこの季節の
限られたこの時刻

三時半過ぎ
大きな樫の木が
ビニールハウスに影を落とすと
ひかりのこどもは去ってゆく
樫の葉っぱとたわむれ遊ぶために
そしてそれから　落日とともに行ってしまう

ロンド
ロンド

さよなら
また あした
回って 回って
また いつか

途上

冬の夕方
中学校の畑の信号のところで
あなた方ふたりに出会う
背がたかくグレーの髪のあなた
ジャンパーにマフラー
手に持つ文庫本
もうひとりの息子らしいひとも
すらりとやせ型で　ジャンパーに手袋
ときどき

彼は飛び跳ねる
ビヨン　ビヨン　と二回続けて
歩道ブロックを踏みはずさない程に

ふたりは　というか　父親は
すこし離れて立っている
息子を見ている
見ているけれど
すこし離れて立っている

そう　この距離だ
信頼の　この距離を得るのに
どのくらいの
暗黒や絶望
日と夜の重ねた学習があったのだろう

家族との距離がわからないの
息子と話せないの　と友が言ったことがある
わたしも
と言って続けられなかった
ほんとうのほんとうを言う言葉が見つけられなくて

信号が変わって渡り
あなた方は　右に曲がってゆく
西へ　西へ
歩道はもう暗いのに
向こうの空は
まだ明るい

ピーナッツ

ピーナッツの種を
蒔いたこと あるかい
種のうちは まだ落花生というのかな

芽はなかなかでてこない
そんなある日 土がほころんで
ちいさな赤ん坊の手が でてくる
それは見てはならないようなおののきだ
きた きた
地の底から やってきた
赤ん坊たちが のびをしながら やってきた

ここは関東ローム層のまんなか
でも　赤土でなく　湿り気をふくむ黒土の地
梅雨どきにも負けず　かれらは黄色い花を咲かせ
花びらが散ったあと　腕をのばし地中にはいりこむ
落花だ
真夏の暑さにも負けず　すがすがしい緑色の葉で
じっと耐え　地の下で成長しつづける
風がちいさな秋をつれてくる
ザクッと　ひとかぶ　掘る
茹でて　いただく
胸いっぱいになる
ここまでおおきくなって食べられてしまって

わたしの畑はちいさいので
冬には　殻付きのピーナッツを買う
血流を良くし　動脈硬化を改善するとか
ところで　さっき　殻をむいたら
ピーナッツの片割れを見失ってしまった

ひとつぶ　それは
赤ん坊　いのち

息

吸って　吸って
ゆっくり　吐いて──
治りにくい肺炎に
ずっとかかっている
けれど
ユーウツや　浅い呼吸はおさらばだ
嫌なことは　外に吐いて
やってゆこう深呼吸
背をのばし　意識を集中させる

昔むかし
海のなかで
一個の細胞ができた
それは多細胞の生物になり
えら呼吸をしだし
大型化し肺呼吸をし陸にあがったという
でも ひとは
今では 肺には
三億の肺胞があるというのに
肺の半分くらいしか使っていないというではないか
ヘイ 了解の了解
自分を燃焼させるんだ
胸だけでなく
お腹をすえてイメージするんだ

空の
海の
すきとおった酸素

とおい
まるいカーブの水平線
深い青い風のひとふきといっしょに
わたしの息は流れてゆく
吸って　吐いて
わたしは　世界を経めぐっていく

雨あがり

林のなかのちいさな川に
ささ舟が浮かんでいた

夜なかに
泣き音もなくふっていたぬか雨
だれかの細い指が
祈りながらつくり浮かべたのだろうか

ところどころ　天をうつす川面
かくれている岩が
網のようなさざ波をはなち

アメンボが
うすい輪っかの水脈をたてている

ふかい沈黙の
キリ　エノキ　ミズナ
風もないのに
ヤマモミジの赤がひとひら落ちた

ああ　そのように
ほんのみじかいあいだ
この岸辺にいて
あなたから落ち流れていってしまった
ちいさないのちよ
もはや　とどまることなく
流れ流れていってほしい

雨があがり
きらめき
揺れて
いっそうのささ舟が
とおい循環の海原へと流れてゆく

ハクモクレン

花が散った　白い花が
陽にかがやいて
まるで白い小鳥が止まっているようだった
風に　枝じゅうの　ちいさな羽が揺れ
さえずりが聞こえてくるようだった

けれど　今
目のまえで
一瞬　パランと　ほどけて散った

喜びも葛藤も　経過も捨て

きのうは　きのう
今までは　今まで
と言うように

あしたは　行ってみよう
白い小鳥が
胸のなかに飛んできたから
もう食べられず筆談になったと聞いて
買ったけれど届けられなかった
軽量の電子辞書をもって
電車で七つ目の
近くて　とても遠い
兄の街

松ぼっくり

五月遅く　海にでかけた
ひと気のまばらな海辺をただ歩きたくて
砂浜につづく松林に
松ぼっくりがころがっていた
大きいの　小さいの
黒いの　茶色いの
丸いの　細いの　楕円形の
こんなにたくさん　この季節にどうして？
ネットの植物図鑑で調べたら
アカマツ　クロマツ

ゴヨウマツ　カラマツ
それぞれ受粉して松ぼっくりが落ちるまで
約一年　一年半　二年など
閉じていた実のヒダが乾いて開いてゆくと
なかの種が風に運ばれてゆく　すると
実は木から落ちるのだそうだが
しばらく落ちないものもあるのだそうだ

窓辺に置かれた松ぼっくり
昨年の猛暑や暴風雨に耐え　風に託した種子
どうやらそんな経緯は文字どおり風化させたらしい
静かな午後
かすかに　傘をひろげた　松ぼっくり
花になろう　また花になろう
と思っているらしくて

ダンゴムシ

日曜日
おおきな公園の道ばたで
こどもたちが
ダンゴムシをみつけた
つまみあげて少しつっつく
ダンッ　丸まってしまう
あっけにとられるほどの素速さ
自由な拒絶
屈託のなさ

もっと　いないかな
いないねぇ
こどもたちは　飽きて走って行ってしまった
うすい陽がななめにさし
影がたたずんでいるそこ
落ち葉のたまり場の下の闇
ダンゴムシはここで生まれたのだろうか
ダンッ　がんこなんです
ダンッ　バイバイです
転がされ　どこに落とされても
また　ゆっくりと　歩いてる

波乗り

海に数人
サーファーがいる

サキは言う　わたしプレートが入っているの
飛び降りて手術されて　生きていて良かった
と今は思っている　あの人は港ではなかったのね
とても不安で悩んでいた普通の人だったのね
まだ心底許せないのだけれど

右に左に　波に乗る
海に数人　サーファーがいる

あの人は顔が無く言葉も無くて
つねられて目を覚まされたとき何かが壊れた
鍵を閉められたとき　隙間から海を見ていた
海って広くて大きくて跡形が無いのがいいな
ひとつ資格取れたから　一度海に出ようかな
跡形も無く　いつか自分も許せたらいいな
右か左か　一瞬に決める
海に数人　サーファーがいる
コロナによる緊急事態宣言が解除された海
その映像が流れている

II

いわし雲

西の空に
いわし雲がひろがっていた
空は　青く高く
雲の端だけ　赤く金色にひかっていた
もう　秋なんだ
季節はゆっくり変わっていたんだ
——ああ
ヒトはヒトから生まれる
雲はなにから生まれるのだろう

もしかしたら　ひみつの涙から？

白いカーテンの
あの部屋
あなたは　いっしょに
矛盾して引き裂かれているわたしや
ちぢこまって言葉をだせなかった幼い頃のわたしを
言葉で育てなおそうとしてくれた
あなたは　そこに居てくれた
わたしは知らなかった自分を発見した
そして　少しだけれど
わたしは変わった

あの冬と

春と夏の
ひみつの涙が
空にのぼったのだろうか
華やかに
とても晴れやかに

夏が過ぎたら
となんとなく思っていた
寂しいけれど　お別れを言う
雲を見たのだから
秋のいわし雲を見たのだから
見たのは　このわたしなのだから

今なら もっと

小さな広場に
紙芝居のおじさんがやってきた
子どもたちは水飴を買ってそれを見た
わたしはあまり買えなくて遠くから見ていた
でも おじさんは
一幕終わったから二幕目からこっちへおいで
と誘ってくれた　いいおじさん
おじさんはミヤタ君のお父さんだ
ミヤタ君を押しては駄目です
怪我したら血が止まらないからと先生が言う

ミヤタ君が転んで教室に来なくなった
先生とお見舞いにいった
おじさんはなんだか小さくなっていた
この障子のすぐ向こうで寝ています
全部聞こえていますから喜んでいます
会わないで帰ってやってください
と玄関でお辞儀をした

紙芝居は激しくなった
ドン　ドン　ドドーン　ドドーン
カッカ　カッカッカー　ドドーン
おじさんは大きく太鼓をたたき声を張りあげ
太い眉に　目も鼻も口も広げ
涙　鼻汁　唾を飛ばして

からだは赤くふくらんではち切れそうで
わたしはただただびっくりしていた
洗面器にたくさんの血を出して
ミヤタ君が亡くなったそうだ
おじさんの紙芝居は見られなくなった
今なら　もっと　水飴を買えるのに
もっと　気持ちがわかるのに

黒い魚

裏山の岩の割れ目の
ちいさな湧き水
マサオはこっそり魚を飼っていた
黒い魚　それをわたしにくれると言う
だれにも言うなよ
母親がいなくなって
父親と海を渡るのだそうだ
夜半すぎに港を出るのだそうだ
父ちゃんと母ちゃんが怒鳴っているとき
押入れで呪文をとなえてた　こわいから

だれにも言うなよ
どしゃ降りの雨が降った
湧き水の池は決壊し魚は泳ぎでた
海峡を　国境を
ひとがつくった境目を
マサオが先か
魚が先か
魚はマサオか
着くところはあるのか無いのか
目をひんむいて
泳ぐ
泳ぐ
夜を泳ぐ

麦

ちいさいころ
麦踏みにつれていかれた
家のまえの丘の　開墾したという畑
なぜか　夕方に　父とふたりだった
早春の土の冷たさが
硬い金属のように長靴の底から射してきた
さわさわ　枯れ草が揺れた
その揺れが伝っていった山の方を見て
「あっちの方で人が死ぬぞ」と父は言った

夕闇が来ていた
草のなかを　なにか獣が歩いているようだった
父は急いで
残り一列の麦の根を踏んでいた

さむいよう
こわいよう

木の枝が揺れ　草がはげしく渦まいた
黒い獣のような塊がそばにやってきた
すると　父はわたしを抱きあげ
片腕をつかみながら　片方の手を伸ばした
ゴオーッと　一直線
ふたりは並んで飛んでいた

もしかしたら
父は歳でもうはしごに登れなかったので
あれはほかの誰かだったのかもしれない
わたしは飛んでいた
未来の
麦のように
光の矢となって

赤い時間

オニヤンマが　わたしのこころを圧倒した
虫かごのなかで
黒と黄のからだ　銀の羽
つやつやの緑いろのおおきな眼を
くるりと　動かして
男の子たちがやっているように
紐をつけて
トンボと一緒に走ってみたいなあ
ひとり留守番をしている夕方だった

わたしは紐を見つけ
なにをしたのか
なにが起こったのか
よくおぼえていない
あたりは　どんどん赤くなった

トンボは
スイーッと飛んで　落下
バタバタ　羽をばたつかせていた

首は
わたしの指　ひとさし指に噛みついていた
巨大な複眼が
赤く染まってにらんでいた
窓も壁も天井も

真っ赤だった

その日　それから
確かに　夕陽が沈み

わたしは生きてきた
かつてふるえた　複眼の恐怖はうすれ
ときどきその他のことで
こころの　深い　割れ目に落ちるが
わたしは生きている

チェリーの頃

日射しが
葉っぱが　濃くなった
お店に
アメリカンチェリーが並んだ
初夏のキッチンで
ジョイスとチェリーを食べた
ジョイスは言った
あなたは自分の価値を低く見すぎているのよ
あなたは　笑顔がいい　　（ありがとう
英語がしゃべれる　　（少しね

コップを洗うのがじょうず　(そんなことも？)
ない
できない
なにもない　と思うとき
ささやくようなジョイスの声
あなたは　いいものを持っているのよ
あまい　おいしい　チェリーよ
やさしいやさしい　チェリーよ
夏のパラソルを開くまえに
胸のなかで
思い出のチェリーが転がってゆく

ヴィヴィール（生きよう）

こびりついた
泥よごれの玄関タイルを
軽快なラテン音楽　サルサに乗って
デッキブラシでこすってやる
〝わたしは　笑うんだ〟
〝わたしは　踊るんだ〟

かつて
アフリカから
奴隷にされて連れてこられた人々のリズムと
統治者の白人たちと

移民のリズムと
混じり合った　サルサ

天気は上々
からだに痛みはない
歯切れよいコンガとギター
トランペット
マーク・アンソニーの響く歌声に合わせれば
ここは
コバルトブルーのカリブ海
夢のように　滑ってゆく　白い帆船
その甲板の上を
わたしは
デッキブラシでこすっている

"で なんのために泣くんだ"
"人生は嬉しいことと悲しいことでできている"

やっと独立を勝ち取った
カリブ海の国々の人たちが
歌って 踊っている

"ヴィヴィール ミ ヴィーダ"
"生きよう 自分の人生を"

人生は一度だけ

インディアン村のごみ缶

インディアン村の二つのごみ缶は傾いて
宙に浮いている
雲も浮いている
真昼間
建物はかしいで
誰もいない　動くものがない
カーンと　音のない真空
パウエル湖の水路をゆくボートの先端
波ひとつない水面
両岸には

濃くうすくストライプの地層の大岩
億年の静寂

ここでは時間というものがない
点のような飛行機にも　コミューンの鳥にも
夜の砂漠のイナズマにも
──静寂が　時間を食べてしまった

霊園
大きな黒い木がくもり空の半分をしめている
それは　ヒトの頭部の影のようだ
二つの子供の彫像が
すこし上を向いて何かを見ながら立っている
その背後の
ひろい空間

不安
恐れ

わたしたちはそのまま
わたしたちは裸のまま　放りだされる
頼りなく　また
妙に小気味よく
カーンと　たった　ひとりで

（奈良原一高写真集、写真展を見て）

テキーラ・ツアー

教会まえからバスは出た
総勢二十五人
地球のあちこちからやってきた人たち

どこまで行っても　青い空
どこまで行っても　赤い丘
そして　一面のリュウゼツラン

テキーラ村
わたしたちは　小さな工場の蒸留タンクを見た
それから　試飲する　塩とレモン

寡黙な酒に　むせながら
次に行くのもテキーラ村　隣の村もテキーラ村
バスのなかの空気はゆるみ
いろんな国のお菓子がまわってくる
若いカップルが
日本の文字についてたずねてきた

日本の文字は三種類
ひらがな　かたかな　漢字
「うわー　すごい　頭がいい」

漢字の一部は　物の形からできている
山はこうなって　山
川はこうなって　川
月も　目も

酔っていたからか夫が
母は乳房が縦になった形　と言ってしまった
口をすべらしてはいけないのに
「えぇえーっ」
ロンドンに住むインドの三人娘が驚いている
「それでは　父は？」とカップルの妻
「おまえ　絵を書くなよ」とカップルの夫
三人娘が笑いだす
「えぇえーっ」
「教えて　教えて　どんな　どんな」
父は解らない　何かの道具からかな
バスのなかは大騒ぎ　妄想してか
女性たちもはやしている

エストニアの夫婦もデンマークの婦人も
あっけらかんと手をたたく

きょうは　ゆかいなガイコツ祭りの日
あしたも　たのしいガイコツ祭りの日
これから一か月　死者を想うガイコツ祭り

バスは走る　死者の日に
素朴で卑猥なわたしたちを乗せて
今　生きているわたしたちを乗せて

どこまで行っても　青い空
どこまで行っても　赤い丘

III

ペダルを踏む

"もっててね
はなさないで"
こどもは全力でペダルを踏みしめた
ベンチの方によろけ　砂場の方によろけ
どうにか進んでいく

"はなしていいよー"
振り返ったとたん
おおきくよろけて自転車はとまってしまった

失敗したのに　こどもは

今　目が輝いて　ほっぺたがふくらんでいる
ずっと電車やザリガニやモグラのことで
頭のなかがいっぱいだったのに

"もう　いっかいー"
よろけよろけ進んでいく
はなびらの散り敷いた
おおきな木の根がデコボコとじゃまする地面を
"はなしていいよー"

とっくに　放していたよ
あっ　信号
こどもは　渡らなかった
倒れながらとまって振り返り手をふった

思いだしたよ　あのころを
うれしさを分けあったこと
それから　それから　もっと深い意味
手を放すこと　それは信じること
もう　いっかい　わたしもペダルを踏もう
放たれて　ペダルを踏もう
すこし休んでその後に

ひらひらと

歯医者の隣の
さびれた店舗が改修され
明るいペンキのちいさな保育園ができた
歩道に面したガラス戸には
遮光シートが貼ってあるが
下から二十センチくらい残されたそこは透明で
ふと　なにかが動いている
ガラスに貼りつくように
あがって　見えなくなって
さがって　床の絨毯に落ちて

足だ　あしうらだ
なんとちいさく　純で　ピンクで　やわらかそう

思わずしゃがんで見ていたら
今度は　おおきな二つの瞳になった
瞳は　じーっと　わたしの瞳を　のぞいている
まばたきもせず不思議な生きものを見るように
やあ　びっくりさせてごめんね
横からもでてきた　おおきな二つの瞳
さらに　保育士さんも横から顔をだし
怒らずにわらってくれた

ふと　なんだね
うれしいものに出会うのは

やはり図書館に行こう　いつか見た
冬の藪から飛びたって行ったいっぴきのシジミ蝶
あのようには飛べないけれど
ひらり　ひらひら
上向いたこころをなびかせながら

スプリング

のっても いいよ
と言うので
アパートの駐輪場の裏道で 立ちどまった
ひつじだった
緑いろの耳と赤い四つの車輪が足についている
ボクのこえ きこえたの うれしいな
ボク あきのはじめから ここにいるの
みーちゃんたちが ひっこししたから
おかあさんと おとうさんと みーちゃんと

さんりんしゃのさんちゃんは　いっしょ
おうちがせまいので　ボクは　はいらないんだって
おかあさんが　ぎゅーしてくれて　おとうさんが
あたまをなでてくれて　ばいばいって
ボク　なんで　どうしてって　わからなくて
ボクが　はやくはしったから　いけなかったのかな
いっぱい　いっぱい　ないたの　みんなきらい
きらいですきで　ないて　ないて　つかれちゃった
でも　ゆうがた　こうもりさんたちが　やってきて
ちゅうがえりこうくうしょーを　みせてくれたの
それから　ちゃいろのはっぱさんが　おりてきたの
ひとりになるのもいいものさ　でもないてもいいよ
ふゆのよるは　おほしたちが　またたいて
くうきだって　きらきらひかるんだ　あさになって
さーっと　いっちゃうんだけど　それから

かぜさんが　ずっとやってきて　ささやいてくれた
いま　ここ　が　だいじさぁ
きみが　いること　が　だいじさぁ
ボク　すこし　おおきくなったよ　のってもいいよ
驚いて　ただ立っていた　乗せてもらえば良かった
今朝　ひつじ君の姿はなく　つつじが満開だった
出発したんだ　きっと

高い空

空から　小さなオナガが落ちてきた
ギギィーッ　ギギィーッ　親鳥は叫び飛びまわるが
ピィ　ピィ　頭が産毛のその子は　飛べない
家のなか　ダンボール箱に止まり木を作り保護した
専門家が　二週間で群れに戻れるでしょうと言うので
ドッグフードを水にふやかし　割り箸の先に載せて
開いたピィの口の中に差し込む　思い切りぐんと喉の
奥に差し込まないと　嘴を閉じる時にこぼしてしまう
ゲェーッてなっちゃうね　と子供たちが言う
夫が青虫を捕まえてきた　ピィにとってはお刺身

翼を広げ　ピィピッ　ピィピッ　と喜ぶ
鳥の夜は早い　私たちの夜も早くなった
テレビは消し　トイレに行くのも身を縮めて歩いた
ピィはミシンや棚の上に飛んでゆけるようになった
九月一日　子供たちが登校する時に　ピィを放した
でも高く飛ばないで　私の後について歩くので困った
オナガの群れがきた　柿の高い枝に止まった
ピィは　低い枝に止まって頭を傾げては見上げていた
そうやって一週間　ピィは群れのなかに入っていった
でも　私が外にいると隣家の高いケヤキから一直線に
飛んできて頭や肩に止まった　もう鳥語が解るらしく
群れの一羽がホウと鳴くとすぐに戻っていった
数日いなくなったり現れたり　でも十月のある日から
全く姿を見せなくなった　とうとう別れがきたのだ

あれから幾年月
晴れ渡った高い空にピィの子供の子供を感じる
もっと高いところから私を包んでいるものを感じる
会って別れた　会えたから別れた　それでいい

五月十七日

ひるごろ
外から帰って　玄関先の鉢植えに水をやっていたら
近所のリウマチをわずらっている知人が通った
お元気そうね
お互いに気をつけましょ
体調をひどく悪くしたひと
西城秀樹はもっと気をつければよかったと言っているそうよ
家に入ったら　正午のニュースで
歌手の西城秀樹さんが亡くなりました　と流れた
びっくりした

会いたいなと思っていると
ばったり　その人と会ったとか
電話をしようかなと思ったとき
その人から電話がかかってきたとか
そんなことって　ときどきある

知らない本を開いたところに
まさに探していた言葉が書いてあったとか
新聞を開いたとたん
それが読みたい記事だったとか
そんなことって　ときどきある

けれど　この事実の符合には本当に驚いた
わたしは　誰かと
わたしは　何かと

意識できないこころの
深いふかーいところで繋がっているらしい
ガラス瓶の　赤いスイートピーが
カクン　と　わたしに顔を向けた

＊　西城秀樹さんは二〇一八年五月十六日午後十一時五十三分に死去された。

光る甲虫

酷暑の夏がすこしうすれ詩を書こうとしてから
二十日　いや一か月近くすぎただろうか
ここに座るとまた　あの甲虫のことが浮かんでくる
あの日の夕がた
窓ガラスを這っていた光る緑色の甲虫について
書けば詩になるような気がした
どこから　きたの？
いつから　ここに？
兆しのような　深い知らせのような　その甲虫
ゆっくり這ってカーテンに届きそう
窓を開けたら羽を出し低くまっすぐな線で飛び去った

うす闇のなか　生まれそうだった詩が一つ飛び去った

ユングは　ある著作で書いている
治療がはかどらない極めて理知的な女性患者のことを
ある夕べ彼女は昨日の夢の中で甲虫が現れたと話した
その時コツコツと音がしたのでユングが窓を開けると
黄金のスカラベ（甲虫）が入ってきた　この非合理な
現実を経験したことで彼女の人格は変容していったと

——わたしも変わりたい　なりたい自分に近づきたい
兆しのような　深い知らせのような
どこから　きたの？
どこまで　ゆくの？

鋭い冬が

心理研究オフィスをあとに
坂を下りてゆく
歩道に沿って植わっているプラタナスの
枯れ葉がいちまい　ゆっくり回りながら落ちた
行くときには目に入らなかったのに
今がその時だ　と誰かの声がしたのだろうか

ふと　靴が踏んで
ガサ　ゴソ　と音がして驚く
そうだ　ずっと以前に聞いた音
ゆるやかな日常にどこかで響いていたこの音

影が長い
車道のほうに伸びている
私はここにいるのに
心のいちぶが伸びているのだろうか
分裂している私
さまよえる私
戦うべきものは何なのだろう
切るべきものは何なのだろう
悲しみと虚無だけが鮮明になって
帰りの電車　本のなかで
私の好きなエリク・エリクソンが言う
アイデンティティというのは

私は私である　ということです
私は私であって私以外の何ものでもない　しかし
単にそれだけではなくて　私がそれをちゃんと感じ
自分の心のなかにはっきり納めることができること

ノコギリの歯のような
鋭い冬が　近づいている
葉が落ち　大空があらわれたら
事の本質がもっとよく見えるのだろうか

＊　河合隼雄著『こころの最終講義』参照

冬のあいだに

ときおり　風が来て
窓ガラスや雨戸をノックし
雪柳やミモザの枝を大きく揺すってゆく
ハクセキレイが一羽　虫を求めて
せわしく地面をつつき飛びまわっている
陽が高くなった
冬は去り　春が来たのだろうか

──あの日　わたしは　台所にいた
耳で外の気配を測りながら　何かしていた
何かしていなければ落ち着かなかった

話し声が止んだ　それから
さっと扉が開いた
目の前に　あなた
ああ　あの顔　なつかしいはにかんだ顔

悲劇なのか喜劇なのか　そのとき
頭がしびれて何年も考えていた言葉が全く消えた
一生を閉じるときにはせめて伝えられるかもしれない言葉
もう圧しない要求しないあなたの気持ちを受け入れる
わたしでも無償の愛に近づけそうだった言葉たちが
うすい空気のなか　全く消えた
ぎくしゃく
とんちんかんな　七言八言のやりとりののち
「じゃ　またね」と照れたようにあなたは去っていった
ぶ厚い氷を砕くハンマーの音もなく　静かに　緩慢に

83

いえ　素速く過ぎたモノクロームの
それは夢？
ほんとうははっきり覚えていない
陽が高くなった　春が来た
わたしはもう戻らない
閉ざされていたながい冬のあいだに
やっと　ひとつの次元を超えられたのだから

「去られるために　そこにいる」

住宅地　雑木林　キャベツ畑を上り
丘に出ると
山々の姿があらわれる
丹沢山塊
大山をまんなかに
遥かかなた
おおきく両腕を広げ　近よってくる
何度　私はこの景色を見に来ただろう
何度　私はここに立ち尽くしただろう

何をどうしたらいいか　反芻しただろう

深夜　本のなかで出会った言葉
「去られるために　そこにいる」
フロイトの娘で心理学者の　アンナ・フロイトが
アメリカに渡る愛弟子エルナ・ファーマンに贈った言葉
母親というものは
去られるためにそこにいる

その言葉に　息がつまった
目の前が反転し　そして　解った
会いに行き　去ってゆく
会いに行き　去ってゆく
その時　ずっと　静かに　そこにいてくれたのは

今日は　空いちめんの綿雲で
山々はうす紫の青色にかすんでいる
この時期とびきり晴れていれば
ほんとに淡くうすく黄緑がかって見えるのに
それは　芽吹き　山々の鼓動
私は　飽きずに見つめ　また去ってゆく
私には無いと思っていた
いつかまた還るところ
ふるさとを感じられた安堵に包まれて

ふきのとう

土手の柿の木の下に
ふきのとうが出はじめた
ひとつ　ふたつ　みっつ
さわやかなきみどり色の
ちいさな頭
どのくらいの間
闇の底にうずくまっていたのだろう
しずかにゆっくり時間をふくらませ
さあ　今　と決めて
地べたをこじあけ出てきた

ふきのとうに　なってみたい
はじめての春の朝を
生まれたてのその眼でまた見られたら
はじめての春の匂いを
胸いっぱいによろこんで吸い込められたら

むっつ　ななつ　にじゅう
やがて土手いっぱいになる
いつか葉っぱはパラボラアンテナのように
ヒトも感じられない
はるかな宇宙の電磁波を受信するのだろう
ちいさなふきのとうは
苦くて　深い

ACKNOWLEDGEMENTS

I decided to publish another collection of poems. It has been almost nine years since my last collection. During that time, disasters caused by climate change are becoming more frequent, and there have been various disasters and sinister incidents. We have experienced the COVID-19 pandemic. Then the war broke out. I have been influenced in no small way by this unstable society. I would like to dedicate this collection of poems to the people who are facing various difficulties on the way in their life, who are trying their best to pull up themselves from hardship and want to start walking again.

    I asked Ms. Christine Hull, my young friend, to check my translation. She is currently involved in supporting and educating underprivileged children in her own country. The two months of English translation exchange were tough but enjoyable, and she gave me many suggestions. One of them was adding a note to the English translation of my poem "If It Was Now" in order to cherish Japan's unique folk culture.

I am deeply grateful.

    I appreciate everybody who read my book.

    Early fall in 2024

                                      Okutsu Sachiyo

Small butterbur sprouts
are bitter and deep

Butterbur Sprouts

Under the persimmon tree on the bank
Butterbur sprouts have started to appear
One, two, three
Like the little heads
of refreshing yellow green

How long have they crouched in the depths of darkness?
They've expanded the time quietly and slowly
and have decided that
it's the time to go
And they've broken open the ground and come out

I want to be like a butterbur sprout
If I could do it,
I can see the first spring morning again with my newborn
    eyes
If I could do it,
I can smell the first spring and happily inhale the scent

Six, seven, twenty
Soon the bank will be full
Someday the leaves will become like parabolic antennas
and probably receive electromagnetic waves we, human
    beings, can't even feel
from far away in space

Who on earth was there still quietly all that time?

Today the sky is full of cotton clouds
The mountains are veiled in a pale purple-blue
If it were exceptionally sunny this time of year,
they would look really pale yellow-green
It's green shoots, heartbeat of the mountains

I gaze away at them without getting tired
and I'll leave again
lapped with the relief I could feel home
which I thought I couldn't do,
which I return to nature

"Mothers Have to Be There to Be Left"

I go up to the residential area, the brush, and the cabbage field
When I get to the hill,
the mountains appear

The Tanzawa Massif
which have Mt. Oyama in the middle
approach me with both open arms
from far away

How many times have I come to see the view?
How many times have I stood still here?
How many times have I wondered what I should do?

In the midnight I encountered the words in a book
"Mothers have to be there to be left"
The words which Freud's daughter, psychologist,
Anna Freud had given her beloved student, Erna Furman,
who had been going to U.S.A.
Mothers have to be there
to be left

I gasped with surprise at the words
Everything in front of me turned over and I understood
Going to see, and leaving
Going to see, and leaving again

     accept your feelings
The words that seemed to bring me closer to unconditional love
absolutely disappeared in the thin air
Awkwardly I apologized for my past by two or three words
After an exchange of seven or eight absurd words,
"See you later," you said shyly and left
There was no sound of a hammer breaking such a thick ice
It passed quietly and slowly
No, it passed quickly and was monochrome
Was it a dream?
I didn't really remember

The sun is getting higher, spring has come
I'll not go back anymore
because I was finally able to transcend one of the dimensions
during the very long winter that was closed

During the Winter

Sometimes the wind comes
and knocks on my window pana or shutters,
shaking the branches of snow off of the willow and mimosa
 violently
A white wagtail pecks the ground
Busily searching for insects
The sun has gotten higher
Has spring come after winter is gone?

--I was in the kitchen that day
I was doing something while listening to the signs outside with
 my ears
I couldn't calm down unless doing something
They stopped talking and then
The door opened quickly
You, in front of me
Ah, your face, the nostalgic shy face of yours

Was it a tragedy or a comedy?
At that time my head was numbed
and my words I had been thinking about for years
disappeared completely
The words that I might at least be able to convey at the end
 of my life
I won't pressure you anymore, I won't demand anything, I'd

Erik Erikson who I like very much says in a book,
"Identity is to say that I am me
I am me and am not someone except me, however,
it is not only merely it
I can feel it properly and hold in my heart clearly"

Sharp winter such as the tooth of the saw
is approaching
When the leaves fall and the sky appears,
Would I see the essence of the things more clearly?

       * Reference, "The Final Lecture of My Heart" by Mr. KAWAI Hayao

A Sharp Winter

I'm going down the slope
after leaving the psychology research office
A dead leaf of the plane trees which were planted along the
 sidewalk
falls turning slowly
Though I didn't catch the sight when I went
Would the leaf hear someone's voice, "Now, it's the time"?

Suddenly my shoes stepped on them
I was surprised to hear a rustling sound
Yes, that's the sound I heard a long time ago
This sound echoed somewhere in my leisurely daily life

My shadow is long
and extends to the roadway
Though I'm here,
I wonder if a part of my heart would extend

I'm divided
I'm wandering
I wonder what I should fight for
I wonder what I should cut
Only sadness and vanity become clear

In the train on my way home

    window
At the moment a golden scarab (beetle) came in
Since she experienced such an irrational reality,
her personality got to change

I want to change too
I want to get closer to who I want to be

Like a sign, like deep news
Where did you come from?
Where do you go?

A Glossy Beetle

I decided to write a poem
since the intense summer heat started to fade a little
It was 20 days or about a month earlier
As I sit here, I remember a beetle again
It would become a poem if I wrote about the glossy green
    beetle,
which was crawling on the window pane
on the evening of the day

Where did you come from?
When did you come here?

Like a sign, like deep news
The beetle was crawling slowly and almost reaching the
    curtains
When I opened the window,
he put out his wings and flew away in a low straight line
A poem that was about to be born flew away in the darkness

C. G. Jung wrote in one of his works
of an extremely intelligent female patient whose therapy was
    not progressing
One evening she told him that a beetle had appeared in her
    dream last night
At that time they heard tapping sounds, so Jung opened the

But I was really amazed at the coincidence of the fact
　　that day

I guess I'm connected up
someone
and something
deep in my mind
that I can't be conscious of

A red sweet pea in a glass bottle
turns toward me quickly

　　　　＊　Mr. SAIJO Hideki passed away at 11:53 p.m. May 16, 2018

May Seventeenth

When around noon I came back from outside
and was watering the potted plants at the side of the front
    door,
an acquaintance of mine
who was suffering from rheumatism in the neighborhood came
    by
"Looks like you're doing well"
"Let's take care of each other"
"A person who has become seriously ill,
SAIJO Hideki, says he should have been more careful"
And when I entered my house, the noon news broadcasted,
"The singer, SAIJO Hideki, has passed away"

I was astonished
When I thought I'd want to see a friend,
I happened to say that I had met the friend at the corner
When I was going to call to a person,
I got a call from the person
That happened to me sometimes

When I opened a new book,
The words I was looking for were written there
When I opened a newspaper,
there was the article I wanted to read
That happened to me sometimes

A flock of azure-winged magpies came
and perched on high branches of persimmon trees
Pie perched on a low branch and tilted her head and looked up
A week passed like that and Pie joined the flock
But when I was outside,
Pie flew straight from the tall zelkova tree next door
to stop on my head or shoulder
Apparently she already understood bird language
When one of the flock cried out, she went right back
Though flock disappeared and appeared for a few weeks,
from that day in October they completely disappeared
It was finally time to say good-by

How many years have passed since then?
I feel a Pie's child's child's child in the clear high sky
And I do something that surrounds me in the high sky
We met and left, we could meet and left
That's fine

The High Sky

A baby azure-winged magpie fell down from the sky
Parent birds flew around with their crying, gigi-gigi
The downy hair bird couldn't fly only chirping, pie-pie

We made perches in a cardboard box in our house to protect
    the baby bird
as experts said the bird would be able to return to a flock
    after two weeks
We soaked dog food in water, placed it on the tip of the
    chopstick,
and inserted it into the baby, Pie's opening mouth
We pushed it as hard as we could into Pie's throat,
otherwise Pie would spill when she closed her beak
My child said while doing it, "I feel like throwing up"
When my husband caught caterpillars like sashimi for Pie,
Pie spread her wings and rejoiced
The bird's night was early so our night became early
We turned off the TV
and tilted our heads when we went to the bathroom
Pie could fly onto the sewing machine and shelves

When my children went to school on September first,
we let Pie loose
I was in trouble because Pie didn't fly high and walked after
    me

In the winter night many stars were twinkling
Even the air was glittering and went out quickly in the
 morning
Then the breeze came and kept whispering to me
"It's important that you live
It's very precious that you stay alive now and here"
I've grown up a little so you could ride me--

I was standing up with surprise; I wish I could ride him
This morning there was no sheep
and azalea trees were in full bloom
I'm sure of his start

The Spring

"You could ride me"
Since I heard a voice,
I stopped on the path behind the bike parking area of the apartment

It was a sheep
which had green ears and four red wheels on his legs

--I'm glad you could hear my voice
I've been here since the beginning of the fall
Because Mi-chan and her family moved to a new house
Mom, Dad, Mi-chan, and the tricycle, San-chan, went together
They said I couldn't go in as the house was too small

Mam gave me a hug and Dad stroked my head
and they said good-by
I didn't know why they hadn't taken me
I guessed it had been my fault that I had run quickly
I cried a lot, I didn't like them
I liked them, I didn't like them, I cried and tired out

But in the evening many bats came
and they showed me their somersault aviation event
Then the brown leaves came down and said,
"It's good to be alone but it's okay you might cry"

I met a happy thing
It came suddenly, didn't it?

After all I'll go to the library
A corbicula butterfly which flew away from a winter bush
Though I can't fly like that,
I'll float with my uplifting heart

With My Uplifting Heart

The deserted store next to the dentist
had been renovated
and a small nursery school painted brightly opened

There was a light shielding sheet attached
to the glass door facing the sidewalk
The part that was left about 20 centimeters from the bottom
    was transparent
Suddenly something was moving
as if it were sticking to the glass
When they went up, they disappeared
When they went down, they fell on the carpet on the floor
Oh, the legs, the bottom of the foot
How tiny, pure, rosy, and so soft they are!

When I crouched down involuntarily and looked at them,
they changed to two big eyes in turn
The eyes were still and gazed about my face
like looking at a mysterious creature without blinking
"Hello, I'm sorry for surprising you"
And another pair of big eyes appeared from the side
In addition the nursery teacher also peeked out from the other
    side
She smiled at me without getting angry

I remembered those days
That we shared the joy
Then it meant something deeper
Letting go meant believing

I'll step on the pedal once again
I'm let go so I'll step on the pedal
After a little rest

I Will Step on the Pedal

"Please, hold here
 Don't let go of my bike"
The child steps on the pedal with all his might
While stumbling toward the bench and the sandbox,
he goes forward somehow

"Let go of my bike"
Even as he turns around,
he stumbles so much and his bike stops

His eyes are shining and his cheeks are puffy now
in spite of his failing,
while his mind has always been occupied
with trains, crayfish and moles

"Once again"
Staggering, he goes on the ground,
which was strewn with petals,
which has been disturbed by large tree roots
"Let go of me"

I've let go of you already
Ah, a traffic signal
He didn't cross
and stopped falling down, turned around and waved

III

dead

The bus runs on the Day of the Dead,
taking us who are simple and obscene
carrying us who are alive now

No matter where we go, the blue sky
No matter where we go, the red hills

The 'moon' like this, the 'eye' like this

Since maybe my husband got drunk,
he said that the character 'mother' was shaped like a vertical breasts
He might not blurt out the story
"What?"
Three Indian girls living in London were surprised
The female of the couple asked, "Then, what is shaped the character 'father'?"
"Hey, don't draw a picture!" the male of the couple said
The three girls burst out laughing

I don't understand, maybe it's shaped from a kind of tool
"Huh?"
"Tell us, tell us, what?, what?"
They made so much noise in the bus
Did they nurse delusion?
Women also said it in perfect unison
An Estonian couple and a Danish lady clapped their hands innocently

Today is the day of the funny Skeleton Festival
Tomorrow would be the day of the fun Skeleton Festival
A month from now: the Skeleton Festival to remember the

A Tequila-Tour

The bus left in front of the church
A total of 25 people
who came from all over the world

No matter where we go, the blue sky
No matter where we go, the red hills
And the field of agaves

In the Tequila Village
we saw distillation tanks of a small factory
And we sampled the drink with the salt and lemon
The reticent hard drink choked up us
The next village we were going to was a Tequila Village
The one after the next one was also a Tequila Village
The air inside the bus was loose
Sweets from various countries turned around
A young couple asked about Japanese characters

There are three types of Japanese characters
Hiragana, Katakana, and Chinese character
"Wow, that's really smart"

Some Chinese characters are made from the shape of things
The character of 'mountain' comes from the mountain shaped
    like this
The character of 'river' comes from the river shaped like this

As Cherries

The sunlight and the leaves
have become deeper
Many stores are showing
American cherries

In early summer
I ate cherries with Joyce in her kitchen
Joyce said,
You underestimate your worth too much
You have nice smiles   (Thank you
You can speak English   (A little
You're good at washing glasses (Even that?

When I feel empty,
When I think I can't do anything,
When I think I have nothing,
Joyce's voice whispers to me
You should know you have something good

Sweet, delicious cherries!
Gentle, tender cherries!

Before I open a summer parasol,
cherries of memories are rolling
in my heart

In a straight line
we were both flying over

Maybe
the person might have been someone else
since my father was too old to climb a ladder anymore

I was flying
in future
like wheat,
like an arrow of light

Wheat

When I was young,
I was taken out for stepping on wheat roots
to the cultivated field on the hill in front of my parents' house

For some reason, it was just my father and I in the evening
The cold of the soil in early spring
shot through the bottom of my boots like hard metal

The dry grasses were swaying
My father looked at the mountain where the swaying spread
and said, "A person will die over there"

The dusk of the evening was coming
It seemed that some beast was walking through the grasses
My father hurriedly stepped
on one remaining row of the wheat roots

I'm cold!
I'm scared!

The tree branches were swaying and the grasses were
    swirling violently
A lump like the black beast came near me
Then my father picked me up
and stretched out his one hand while catching my one arm

and swam
Swam, swam
the night

A Black Fish

A small spring
from the crack of the rock of the mountain
Masao had secretly kept a fish in it
A black fish, he told me that he would give it to me
"Don't tell anyone!"

Since his mother was gone,
apparently he and his father were going to cross the sea
they would leave the port after midnight
"When Mom and Dad were yelling,
I was chanting an incantation in the closet"
"Because it's scary"
"Don't tell anyone!"

A big downpour came
The spring pond burst
and the fish swam out and got over
The strait, the border
The boundary human made

Was Masao the first to go?
Or was the fish the first to go?
Was the fish Masao?
Could he arrive somewhere or not?
He tore his eyelids

Kakka Kakkakka Dodoon
The guy beat the drum loudly and raised his voice
His thick eyebrows went up and down
He widened his eyes, nose, and mouth
and flew tears, nasal mucus, and saliva
His red body swelled up and looked like it was going to burst
I was just surprised

It seemed that MIYATA-kun had passed away
after lots of bleeding into the washbowl
I could no longer watch the guy's picture-story show
If it was now, I could buy more starch syrup
If it was now, I could understand his feelings more

> * 'kamisibai' is a traditional Japanese theatrical. The performer took out many pictures that depicted scenes from the story in sequence and dramatically explained them. Usually he sold sweets in exchange for performance on the street.

If It Was Now

The picture-story show (kamisibai)* guy had arrived
at the small square
The children bought starch syrup and watched the show
I watch the show from a distance because I was not able to
    buy it too much
But the guy invited me,
"The first act is over, so come here for the second one"
He was a good person!

He was MIYATA-kun's father
Our teacher said, "Don't push MIYATA-kun
If he got injured, his bleeding wouldn't stop"

MIYATA-kun fell and stopped coming to our class
The teacher and students went to see the MIYATA's house
The guy seemed to be getting smaller
"My son lies right next to this shoji screen
And he's happy because he can hear everything
Please go home without meeting him"
He said his thanks and bowed at the entrance

The picture-story show became more intense
Don Don Dodoon Dodoon

in the winter,
spring and summer,
gorgeously,
so brightly

Somehow, I thought
I would say when the summer passed away
Though I feel lonely,
I'll say good-by

Because I saw a cloud
Because I saw the autumn sardine cloud
Because it was me who saw it

A Mackerel Sky

In the western sky
sardine clouds are spreading
The sky is high and blue
And only the edges of the clouds are red and golden

Autumn has already come
The season is changing step by step

― Ah,
   Humans are borne by humans
   What are clouds borne by?
   Are they borne by secret tears?

In the room
with white curtains
you sympathized with me
and tried to raise me up
because I had been torn apart by contradiction
and had shriveled so scared to speak in my childhood

You were there
I discovered something about myself that I hadn't known
And I changed a little bit

Would secret tears go up to the sky?

II

There are several surfers in the sea

The TV networks televise the sea
where the state of emergency due to corona virus has been
    lifted

Surfing

There are several surfers
in the sea

Saki says,
"I have a plate in my body
I was glad to be alive after jumping off and having surgery
Now I think I was lucky but that person was not a harbor for
 me
She was just a normal one who was very anxious and worried
I still can't forgive her from my heart, though"

Riding on the waves to the right and left
There are several surfers in the sea

"The person has no face and no words
Something was broken in my heart when I was woken up by
 her pinch
I gazed away at the sea through the gap of the wall when she
 locked me in
I love that the sea is wide and big besides it leaves nothing
Since I got a qualification for the job, I'll try surfing once
I hope I could forgive her and myself without a trace
 someday"

Deciding the moment to the right or left

They seem to think
let's become a flower, let's become a flower again

Pine Cones

I went to the sea in late May
I just wanted to walk along the deserted coastline
There were pine cones left in the forest leading to the beach
The big one, the small one
The black one, the brown one
The round one, the thin one, the oval one
Why were there so many in this season?

I checked it in an online plant encyclopedia
Japanese red pine, Japanese black pine
Japanese white pine, Larch
It seemed to take about a year, a year and a half or two
    years,
until each pine cone pollinates and falls off
When the closed folds of the fruit dry up and open up,
the seeds inside are carried away by the wind
And it looks like it's actually falling from the tree
But some cones don't seem to fall off for a while

Pine cones placed by the window
Seeds that withstood intense heat and rainstorms of last
    year and entrusted the wind
Apparently they have weathered the memories away
In the quiet afternoon
they spread their umbrellas slightly

The city my brother lives in
is the seventh stop on the train
It's so close and so far

The Magnolia Denudata

The flowers were scattered
The white flowers
They were shining in the sun
and looked like small white birds were perching on
Their little feathers all over the branches were swaying in the wind
It seemed like I could hear chirping

But now
in front of my eyes
in a moment
they untangle and drop

As they say
throw away joy, conflict and process,
yesterday is yesterday
the past is the past

I'll go tomorrow
since a little white bird flew into my heart

With a lightweight electronic dictionary
I bought
when I heard he couldn't eat anything,
couldn't talk and had to communicate by writing

Transparent oxygen
in the sky
in the sea

The distant round curved horizon
My breath flows
with a puff of deep blue wind

Breathe, spit
I'll travel through the world

Breath

Breathe, breathe
Spit it out slowly

I've been suffering from pneumonia
that is difficult to cure
However,
I'll say good-by to depression and shallow breathing
and spit out the things I don't like
Let's take a deep breath

I'll stretch my back and concentrate my attention
It is said
once upon a time
one cell was formed in the sea
And it became a multicultural organism,
Started breathing with gills, became more larger,
breathed with lungs and ascended the land
But
I heard human beings only use about a half of their lungs,
even though currently there are 300 million alveoli in

Hey, I get it!
I'll fill my heart with pattion
I'll concentrate my image on my stomach
more than I breathe with my chest

They grow up so big and get eaten

As my field is small,
I usually buy in-shell peanuts in the winter
It is said that they improve blood flow and arteriosclerosis
By the way, just now I peeled off their shell
And I lost a tally of peanuts

Even a peanut is
a baby, a life

Peanuts

Have you ever sown peanut seeds?
I guess it's still called a RAKKASEI when it's a seed

Buds don't appear easily
Like one day, the soil is loosened
and a little baby's hand comes out
That's quake that we shouldn't see
Come out, come out
Babies come out with stretching
from the depth of the earth

Here is the middle of loamy layer of the Kanto Plain
But it's not red soil, it's black one with the moisture
Despite the rainy season, they bloom yellow flowers
After the petals fall down, the cores stretch their arms into
    the ground
It's called RAKKA, which means the falling flowers
Despite the midsummer heat, they endure fixedly
with refreshing green leaves
and continue to grow under the ground

The wind brings the cool autumn
I dig peanuts
I boil and eat them
My heart feels sad

you got

My friend once told me,
"I don't know how to measure a distance from my family"
"I can't talk to my son"
I said, "me too"
But I didn't continue speaking
As I couldn't find the words to say the truth

We cross the roadway after the lights change
You two turn to the right
to the west, to the west
Though the sidewalk is already dark,
the sky over there
is still bright

On the Way

In the evening of the winter day
I meet you two
at the traffic light near the field of the junior high school

You are tall and have gray hair
and wear a jumper and muffler
and have a pocketbook

Another person who seems to be your son
is also slender and thin
and wears a jumper with gloves
Sometimes
he jumps two times
without leaping off of the sidewalk

You two or rather I should say
you, the father, are standing a little further away
and watch your son
Though you watch him,
you are standing to distance yourself from him

Yes, the distance is!
The distance of trust building
I wonder how many days and nights
of darkness, despair and learning

from the roof of the plastic greenhouse and
from the ledge of one

This limited time
of this fragrant season
opening my window

After three thirty p.m.
when a big oak tree
casts the shadow on the greenhouse,
the children of the light are going back
to play with the oak leaves
And then they go away with the setting sun

Rondo
Rondo

Good bye
See you tomorrow
Turn around, turn around
See you someday

Rondo

In pain
I'm lying on the sofa
Then in the afternoon

Heat haze-like
faint lights are coming
They ripple and get darker
They stretch or shrink
The children of the light of parallel-striped pattern

The walls become brighter
The outline of each face
of the old radio on the shelf and the wall clock
come to life
clearly

In this winter
my neighbor built a plastic greenhouse of the semi cylinder
    type
at the boundary of the land of south side
My view was blocked
and I couldn't see the small trees in the park anymore

The children of the light
who came straight
without constraint

I

Contents

I

Rondo 141
On the Way 139
Peanuts 137
Breath 135
The Magnolia Denudata 133
Pine Cones 131
Surfing 129

II

A Mackerel Sky 125
If It Was Now 123
A Black Fish 121
Wheat 119
As Cherries 117
A Tequila-Tour 116

III

I Will Step on the Pedal 111
With My Uplifting Heart 109
The Spring 107
The High Sky 105
May Seventeenth 103
A Glossy Beetle 101
A Sharp Winter 99
During the Winter 97
"Mothers Have to Be There to Be Left" 95
Butterbur Sprouts 93

ACKNOWLEDGEMENTS 91

To Be Left and to Leave
(The Abstract of 23 Poems)

あとがき

また詩集を出そうと思いました。前詩集から九年近く。その間、気候変動による災害が頻発し、様々な事故や陰湿な事件がありました。コロナウイルスによるパンデミックや、戦争が起きました。この不安な社会は少なからず私の人生にも影響しました。この詩集は、人生の途上で、様々な困難とぶつかりながら、崩れそうになる気持ちを一生懸命に引き締めて、またもう一度と歩き出そうとしている人に捧げたいと思います。

翻訳チェックは、現在自国で恵まれない子供たちの支援や教育にたずさわっている若き友人のクリスティーン・フルさんにお願いしました。英訳交換の約二か月は厳しくも楽しい時間で、彼女から様々な提案を戴きまし

た。その一つ、日本独自の庶民文化を大切にするため、詩「今なら　もっと」の英訳に注釈を付けました。深く感謝致します。

作品は、詩誌「竜骨」、「いのちの籠」、「こだま」、「回游」、月刊誌「詩と思想」に発表したものから選びました。詩集を編むに際しまして、「竜骨」主宰の高橋次夫様より高潔な助言を戴きました。記して感謝致します。

出版にあたり、土曜美術社出版販売の高木祐子様に、暖かくて的確な支援を戴きました。厚くお礼を申し上げます。スタッフの皆様に感謝致します。

読んでいただいた皆様に感謝致します。

二〇二四年　秋海棠の頃

奥津さちよ

著者略歴

奥津さちよ（おくつ・さちよ）

横浜市に生まれる

1986 年　詩集『例えば地球を転がしてみたり』（レアリテの会）
1988 年　詩集『円周率が駆けてくる』（レアリテの会）
1991 年　詩集『揺れるすべり台』（レアリテの会）
1998 年　詩集『ハンス』（詩学社）
2007 年　詩集『窓の外を』（編集工房ノア）
2015 年　詩集『歩く』（土曜美術社出版販売）

現住所　〒245-0013 横浜市泉区中田東 4-59-8
E メール　sachipoe@yahoo.co.jp

OKUTSU Sachiyo

Born in Yokohama, Japan

1986 Published the poetry "If I Tried to Roll the Earth"
1988 "The Circular Constant Comes Running"
1991 "The Waving Chute"
1998 "Hanse"
2007 "Outside of My Window"
2015 "I Walk"

Address　4-59-8 Nakata-higashi, Izumi-ku, Yokohama-shi,
　　　　　Japan 245-0013
E-mail　sachipoe@yahoo.co.jp

詩集　去られるために　去るために
発　行　2024年11月15日

著　者　奥津さちよ
装　幀　直井和夫
発行者　高木祐子
発行所　土曜美術社出版販売
　　　　〒162-0813　東京都新宿区東五軒町 3-10
　　　　電　話　03-5229-0730
　　　　ＦＡＸ　03-5229-0732
　　　　振　替　00160-9-756909
ＤＴＰ　直井デザイン室
印刷・製本　モリモト印刷

Publisher　Takagi Yuko
Publishing office DOYO BIJUTSUSHA SHUPPAN HANBAI
Adress　3-10, Higashigoken-cho, Shinjuku-ku Tokyo, Japan 162-0813
Tel 03-5229-0730
E-mail doyobi@vc-net.ne.jp
URL https://userweb.vc-net.ne.jp/doyobi/index.html
ISBN978-4-8120-2873-5　C0092

ⓒ OKUTSU Sachiyo 2024, Printed in Japan